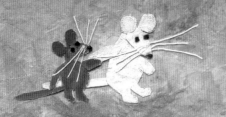

TO LONNIE,

FOR WHOM MY LOVE IS GREATER
THAN ANY WORDS AND BIGGER THAN ANY NUMBERS,
AND ALL OF THESE TOGETHER, FOREVER.

Published by Dial Books for Young Readers
A Division of Penguin Books USA Inc.
375 Hudson Street
New York, New York 10014

Designed by Ann Finnell
Printed in Hong Kong
First Edition
3 5 7 9 10 8 6 4 2

Library of Congress Cataloging in Publication Data
Roth, Susan L.
My love for you / Susan L. Roth. —1st ed.
p.   cm.
Summary: Two mice walk along comparing love
to animals from one bear to ten lovebirds.
ISBN 0-8037-2031-9 (tr.). —ISBN 0-8037-2032-7 (lib. bdg.)
[1. Love—Fiction. 2. Mice—Fiction. 3. Counting.] I. Title.
PZ7.R737My 1997 [E]—dc20 95-53759 CIP AC

To make these collages I used many thin papers, some thicker papers,
glue, scissors, tweezers, and a little paint for the mice.—S.L.R.

My Love for You

Susan L. Roth

DIAL BOOKS FOR YOUNG READERS
NEW YORK

MY LOVE FOR YOU...

IS BIGGER THAN **1** BEAR,

TALLER
THAN
2 GIRAFFES,

LARGER THAN **3** BLUE WHALES,

WIDER THAN **4** ELEPHANTS,

LONGER

THAN

5 PYTHONS.

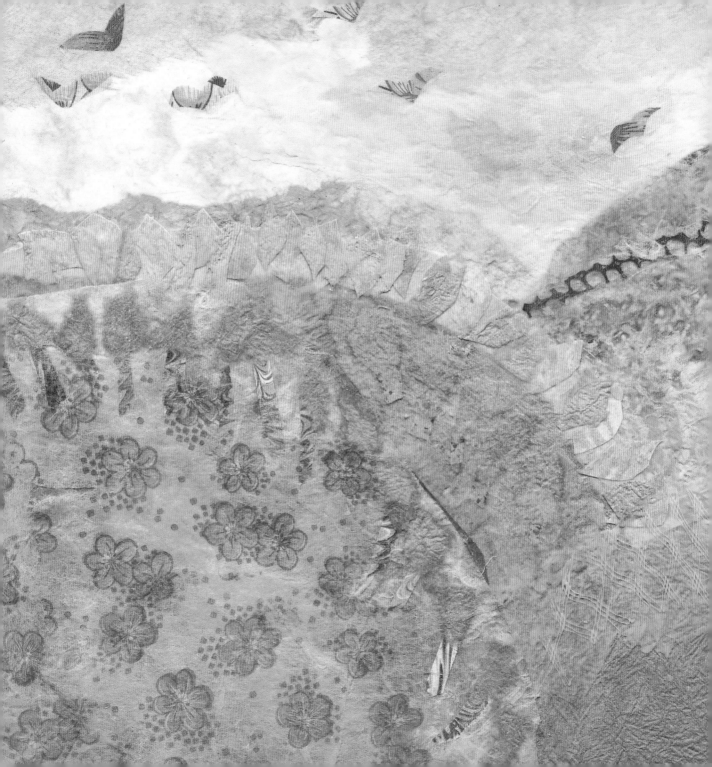

MY LOVE FOR YOU. . .

IS DEEPER

THAN

6 DEEP-SEA FISH,

STRONGER
THAN
7 GORILLAS,

MIGHTIER THAN 8 LIONS,

HEFTIER THAN **9** HIPPOS.

MY LOVE FOR YOU. . .

SOARING HIGH ABOVE THE CLOUDS,

AND GREATER THAN
ALL OF THESE TOGETHER . . .

FOREVER.